The Royal Baby's Big Red Bus

TOUR OF
LONDON

by
Martha Mumford

illustrated by
Ada Grey

BLOOMSBURY

LONDON OXFORD NEW YORK NEW DELHI SYDNEY

It was a beautiful summer's day and the
Royal Family was taking a well earned rest.

The Royal Baby Prince and Princess splashed around gleefully in the royal paddling pool (which was a little bigger than your average-sized pool!).

And everything was calm and peaceful until . . .

The Palace gates opened and a big
red bus rolled up the long driveway.
"All aboard for the Big Red Bus
Tour of London!"
called the driver.

BEEEEEP!

"Perfect timing," they all said
to Driver James.

"Well, come on everyone, what are
you waiting for? All aboard!
Let's have a right royal
fun day out!"

"Cook!" called the Royal Babies' auntie. "We need some hampers, as quickly as you can."

"Nanny Rose, can you bring Royal Baby Prince's dinosaur and Royal Baby Princess's fluffy bunny. We can't leave without them," said the Duchess.

"Can someone bring my binoculars?"
said the Duke.

Finally, everyone (and everything!) was on board.
DING-A-LING-LING! They were off!

DING-A-LING!
"First stop, the Natural History Museum!"
called Driver James. Royal Baby Prince
couldn't believe it! He LOVED dinosaurs.

"Look at all these bones,"
said the Duke.
"They're millions of years old."

"Raaaah! I'm a T. rex," roared the Royal Baby Prince right in his baby sister's face, which she didn't like one little bit.

Waaaaaaah!

DING-A-LING!

The big red bus was off again and the next stop
was ZSL London Zoo. The meerkats made
the Royal Baby Princess laugh.

And EVERYONE agreed the funniest creatures were the penguins at Penguin Beach!

After a delicious picnic lunch in Regent's Park, it was time for the big red bus to roll again — all the way to . . .

DING-A-LING!

The British Museum.
"You can learn all sorts of interesting things about
history here," said the Royal Babies' grandad.
The Royal Baby Prince, however, was far more
interested in the colouring in (and so was
the Royal Baby Princess!).

Beep!
Beep! The big red bus rolled past

the National Portrait Gallery,

Trafalgar Square

and Nelson's Column

. . . before Driver James said,
"Everybody off! It's time for my break."
So they decided on a different
way to travel . . .

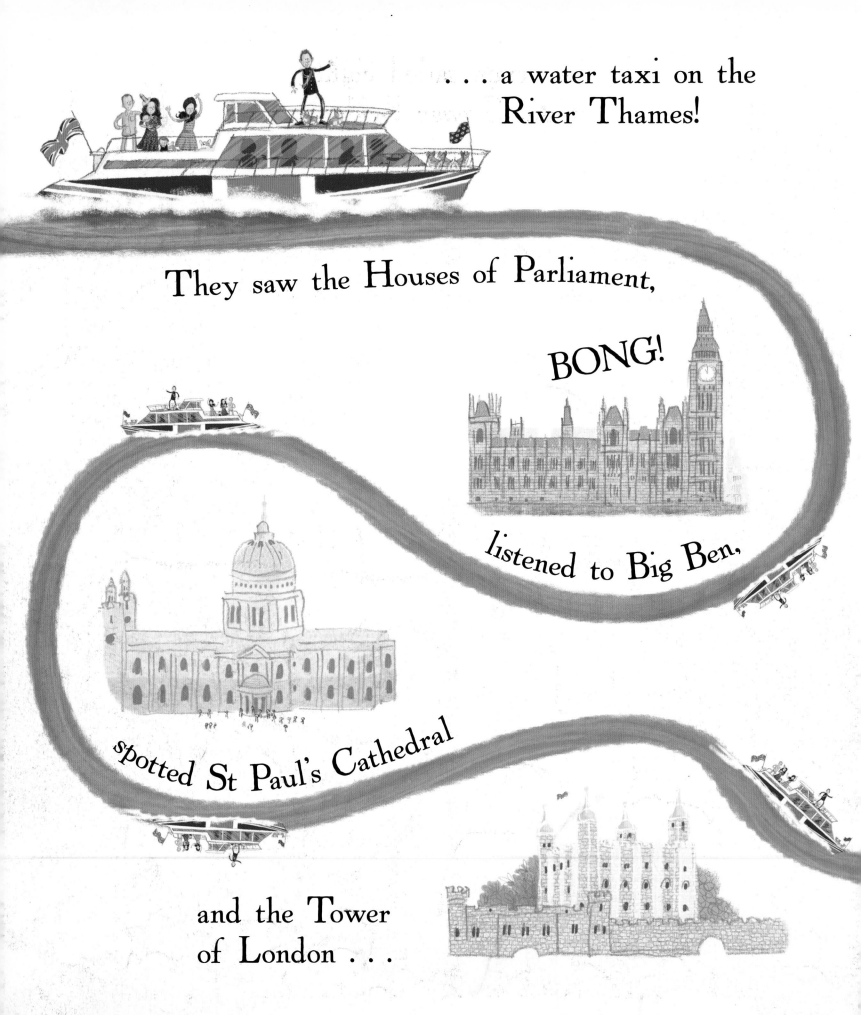

. . . a water taxi on the River Thames!

They saw the Houses of Parliament,

BONG!

listened to Big Ben,

spotted St Paul's Cathedral

and the Tower of London . . .

and even sailed right
under Tower Bridge!

Soon they were in Greenwich, to see the
Royal Observatory and the Planetarium.

"If you look closely, you'll be able to
see a great big bear in the sky," said the Duke.

The Royal Baby Prince couldn't believe his eyes!
It looked a bit like his favourite teddy, Threadbear.

"Come on,"
called the Royal Babies' uncle.
"It's my favourite next —
the London Eye.
We'll be able to see
the WHOLE of London
when we ride on it."

Everyone piled into a capsule.
It was brilliant. "Look!" said the Royal
Babies' grandma. "There's the Shard!"
"And there's the Gherkin!"

When they got out, the Royal
Babies' auntie said excitedly,
"Now it's time for my
favourite thing — shopping!"

The big red bus stopped at all the famous
stores in London — Harrods, Selfridges,
Liberty and, best of all . . .

Hamleys.
It was the biggest toy shop the Royal Babies
had EVER seen. They had so much fun
playing with all the toys . . . mostly!

But then it was goodbye to the
toys and they chugged all the
way back to Buckingham
Palace for tea.

Beep!
Beep!

"Did you have a good day?" asked the Royal Babies' uncle. The Royal Baby Prince and Princess nodded enthusiastically.

The babies' auntie asked, "And did Fluffy Rabbit have a fun time too? I bet she did."

Suddenly, Royal Baby Prince burst into tears. Where was his toy dinosaur? It was missing!

"He can't go to bed without his toy dinosaur," fretted the Duke. "What are we going to do?"

"Leave this to me," said the Duchess.

And she rushed off . . .

All over . . .

everywhere . . .

looking for the dinosaur . . .

And got back —
just in time for bed.

That night, everyone slept happily — especially Royal Baby Prince, Royal Baby Princess, Fluffy Rabbit . . .

and Dinosaur.

For Polly and Kristina – MM
For Ava – my best princess xx – AG

Bloomsbury Publishing, London, New York, New Delhi and Sydney

First published in Great Britain in 2016 by Bloomsbury Publishing Plc
50 Bedford Square, London, WC1B 3DP

A CIP catalogue record for this book is available from the British Library

ISBN 978 1 4088 6896 6 (PB)

Printed in China by Leo Paper Products, Heshan, Guangdong

1 3 5 7 9 10 8 6 4 2

All papers used by Bloomsbury Publishing are natural, recyclable products made
from wood grown in well managed forests. The manufacturing processes conform
to the environmental regulations of the country of origin

www.bloomsbury.com

BLOOMSBURY is a registered trademark of Bloomsbury Publishing Plc